✳ Smithsonian

SYRETIA and the CURIOSITY ROVER

BY AILYNN COLLINS

ILLUSTRATED BY PAULA ZORITE

STONE ARCH BOOKS
a capstone imprint

Published by Stone Arch Books,
an imprint of Capstone.
1710 Roe Crest Drive
North Mankato, Minnesota 56003
capstonepub.com

The name of the Smithsonian Institution and the sunburst logo are
registered trademarks of the Smithsonian Institution. For more information,
please visit www.si.edu.

Library of Congress Cataloging-in-Publication Data
Names: Collins, Ailynn, 1964– author. | Zorite, Paula, illustrator.
Title: Syretia and the Curiosity rover / by Ailynn Collins ; illustrated
by Paula Zorite.
Description: North Mankato, Minnesota : Stone Arch Books, an imprint of Capstone,
[2022] | Series: Smithsonian historical fiction | Audience: Ages 8–11. | Audience: Grades
4–6. | Summary: Having just moved to California, Syretia's mother enrolls her and
her younger brother, Sean, in the only summer camp available: Mars or Bust, which
is focusing on the Mars Curiosity rover due to land soon; Sean is thrilled by all things
involving space, but eleven-year-old rock enthusiast Syretia is not really interested,
until she discovers that the rover will be studying Martian geology—as Syretia's team
works on their end-of-camp project, and the hour for the Mars landing approaches,
she finds herself caught up in the excitement and anticipation.
Identifiers: LCCN 2021030686 (print) | LCCN 2021030687 (ebook) |
ISBN 9781663911964 (hardcover) | ISBN 9781663921352 (paperback) |
ISBN 9781663911971 (pdf)
Subjects: LCSH: Curiosity (Spacecraft)—Juvenile fiction. | Science
camps—Juvenile fiction. | Brothers and sisters—Juvenile fiction. |
friendship—Juvenile fiction. | Mars (Planet)—Exploration—Juvenile
fiction. | California—Juvenile fiction. | CYAC: Curiosity (Spacecraft)—Fiction. | Mars
(Planet)—Exploration—Fiction. | Camps—Fiction. | Brothers and sisters—Fiction. |
Friendship—Fiction. | Racially mixed people—Fiction. | California—Fiction.
Classification: LCC PZ7.1.C64472 Sy 2022 (print) | LCC PZ7.1.C64472 (ebook) |
DDC 813.6 [Fic]—dc23
LC record available at https://lccn.loc.gov/2021030686
LC ebook record available at https://lccn.loc.gov/2021030687

Designer: Sarah Bennett

Our very special thanks to Matthew Shindell, Curator, Planetary Science and
Exploration, Space History Department, National Air and Space Museum. Capstone
would also like to thank Kealy Gordon, Product Development Manager, and the
following at Smithsonian Enterprises: Jill Corcoran, Director of Licensed Publishing;
Brigid Ferraro, Vice President of Business Development and Licensing; and Carol
LeBlanc, President, Smithsonian Enterprises.

TABLE OF CONTENTS

Chapter One

Summer Camp Crash Landing

Eleven-year-old Syretia Ma watched her mom drive away with the other parents.

"This is going to be so great," said her younger brother, Sean.

Looking around, Syretia couldn't have disagreed more. Her family had just moved to California from Washington state last week. Mom thought going to an overnight summer camp near their new neighborhood would be a great way to make friends. But this camp was about space. While Sean loved everything about rockets and planets, Syretia would've preferred a camp about geology and rocks—*her* favorite subject. Unfortunately, this camp was the only one available.

Even worse, the "campsite" wasn't really a campsite at all. It was a large, one-story, reddish-brown building surrounded by sports fields. How disappointing. Syretia was used to summer camps being in forests with log cabins. This one was like being back in school!

A young woman stepped up to greet the campers. She wore a bright-orange T-shirt with the words STEM IS MY SUPERPOWER printed across the front.

"What's STEM?" Syretia whispered to Sean.

He rolled his eyes. "Science, technology, engineering, and math. Everyone knows that."

Syretia didn't.

"Welcome to camp, everyone," the woman in the orange shirt said cheerfully. "My name

is Brenda, and I'm the head counselor. I'm very excited to meet you."

Other counselors, also dressed in orange, led the campers around to the back of the building. Brenda gestured toward a line of small, boxy buildings that resembled the temporary classrooms at Syretia's old school. Each had two large windows and a bright-blue door. On every door hung a large poster of a planet—Mercury, Earth, Saturn, Venus, and Jupiter.

"Five planets for five cabins," said a male counselor with bright-blue hair.

"I've assigned twelve kids and a counselor to each cabin," Brenda continued. "You'll find the assembly hall is in the cafeteria in the main building."

She squinted at the clipboard in her hands. "Sy . . . ree . . . tee . . . ah Ma?"

"It's pronounced 'Ser–sha,'" Sean corrected

Brenda. "Lots of people can't say it right because of the weird spelling."

Syretia hated it when her little brother explained her name to people.

"I'm sorry, Syretia," Brenda said. "Now that we all know how to say it, we won't get it wrong again."

"It's okay," Syretia lied. She was named after her Irish grandmother—her mom's mom. And she was used to people saying it wrong. Even her dad's mom—who was Chinese—liked to call her *jie jie*, meaning "big sister," instead.

Syretia was assigned to cabin Mercury, and Sean was headed to Jupiter. As she stepped into her cabin, she was surprised to see how nice it actually was. Bunk beds and twinkle lights lined the length of the pod.

One by one, girls streamed into the cabin. Many of them seemed to know each other from years before. They claimed their beds, wanting to stay next to an old camp friend, or beside the "best" window. Syretia was left with the upper bunk of the bed closest to the door.

As she unpacked, Syretia's heart raced. She felt nervous about the next two weeks and wished she was back in Seattle. She'd had plans with her friends. But life had changed almost overnight after their parents' divorce.

As soon as they'd unpacked, a bell rang. Syretia followed the other girls to the cafeteria. The large room was full of kids laughing and talking all at once. Long dining tables had been arranged in rows, and Syretia found a spot at the very back with the quietest kids. She guessed that they were all new, like her.

She searched the room for her brother. He was up front, laughing with a group of boys like they were old friends. Syretia felt so alone.

At the front of the room, ten counselors in matching orange shirts beamed out at the campers. Brenda blew a whistle. The campers instantly went quiet, and all eyes were on her.

"Welcome to STEM Camp 2012," she said through a headset microphone. Some kids cheered. She pointed at them and smiled. "This year's theme is . . ."

"Mars or Bust!" all the other counselors chorused. Then they whooped and applauded, which made the campers do the same. Syretia clapped politely. She didn't see why this was so exciting.

"You got it!" Brenda said. "We have some great surprises for you, including a visit from two special people."

"Who are they?" someone called out from up front.

Brenda laughed. "First things first—we're going to split you up into small teams. Each team will work together for the next two weeks. You'll create several STEM projects that are related to our theme, including the Grand Project that you'll present at the end of camp." Brenda pointed to the blue-haired counselor who was holding a computer tablet. "Tony here will call your groups. You may not know your teammates now, but by the end of camp, you'll have made some great friends for life."

The campers cheered. Syretia just felt nervous. She wasn't good at making new friends. Tony called out names in groups of three or four. Kids got out of their seats and gathered together with their new teammates. With each name called, Syretia's throat tightened. Sean was put in a group with three other boys. They bumped fists and then sat down together.

"Syretia Ma." Tony looked at her. "You're in a group with Cal and Rhea Morgan."

A tall girl with two long pigtails jumped up and skipped toward Syretia. At the same time, an equally tall boy appeared at Syretia's side.

Cal and Rhea had the same dark-brown hair and infectious smiles.

"Hi! I'm Rhea. And this is my twin brother, Callisto. And yes, I'm named after a moon of Saturn, and Cal after one of Jupiter's," Rhea explained, as if Syretia would have already guessed that.

"What does your name mean?" Cal asked eagerly.

"I don't know." Syretia shrugged. "It's just my grandmother's name."

"No worries," Rhea said, pulling a tattered book out of her backpack "I carry a book of names for this very purpose."

"It's weird, I know," Cal added. "But it's something Rhea loves to do."

Rhea flipped through her name book. "S-Y-R . . ." she mumbled. "Aha! It says that *Syretia* means 'curious one.'" Her eyes widened, and a grin spread across her brother's face.

"We are so going to win the Grand Project this year!" Rhea shrieked.

"It's practically written in our names!" Cal clapped.

Syretia looked at her new teammates, her brows knitted tightly together.

Rhea wrapped her arm around Syretia's shoulders as if they were best friends. "Don't you get it? I heard this camp is focusing on a Mars rover called Curiosity."

"So, it's like the universe put us together," Cal finished. "Think about it, Syretia—you're the Curious one, right? Like Curiosity?"

As the twins chatted about being the best team ever, Syretia said nothing. She wasn't sure about Rhea and Cal's excitement, or the camp theme, or even what a rover was. She had a sinking feeling that she wouldn't be able to help with any of their projects.

This camp was going to be a disaster.

Chapter Two

A Girl Like Me

The next morning, Syretia awoke to Brenda's overly cheerful voice. The counselor handed each girl an orange T-shirt, like the one she was wearing.

"You don't have to wear them at camp," Brenda said. "But they'll remind you of the fun times we had here after you leave."

Syretia began to put her shirt away. But then she noticed the other girls slipping into the new shirts. She reluctantly took off her *Geology Rocks!* tee and put on the orange shirt.

At breakfast, the cafeteria was a blinding sea of orange.

"Sit with us, Curiosity girl." Rhea appeared beside Syretia. She carried a tray piled high with food. "I've got enough for our team."

Cal arrived with three glasses of juice. Syretia quickly gulped hers down, which made her feel a little better.

All through breakfast, Rhea chatted as Syretia listened. When all the food was gone, and the trays returned to the kitchen, the microphone screeched. All heads turned to the front of the cafeteria. A large screen unrolled from the ceiling as Brenda spoke.

"We have a special treat for you to start off our camp theme." She bounced with excitement. "As you may know, during our camp, NASA's latest rover will land on Mars. What's it called?"

"Curiosity!" everyone shouted back.

Brenda grinned proudly. "That's right! Curiosity was launched last November. It has traveled across space for the past eight months. When it lands, it will give us so much more information about the Red Planet."

"What exactly is a rover?" Syretia leaned over to ask Cal.

Cal's eyes almost popped out of his head. "Where have you been?" he said.

Rhea glared at her brother. "A rover is a robotic vehicle with all kinds of scientific equipment attached. It's used to explore places people can't go. It collects and records information and sends it back to scientists on Earth," she whispered.

"The Curiosity rover will help us learn about Mars," Cal added. "Since we can't send astronauts there—at least not yet."

"Some of you may be wondering how the rover got its name," Brenda continued. "Well, in 2009, a contest was held. The finalists included names like *Adventure*, *Pursuit*, and *Wonder*, but the winner was *Curiosity*. Does anyone know who thought of that name?"

Syretia heard murmurs among the campers but couldn't make out what they were saying.

"Wasn't the contest winner a sixth grader at the time?" a boy from Sean's team finally called out.

"That's right," Brenda said. "Her name is Clara Ma, and we're going to video chat with her in a few minutes."

The campers whooped and cheered.

"That's cool!" Cal said, turning to Syretia. "She has the same last name as you. Do you know her?"

Syretia shook her head and shrugged. But it *was* interesting. A girl, about her age and with the same last name, had named the rover? That was pretty cool.

The screen came on and Syretia's eyes were fixed on the face of a teenage girl. She had straight black hair and dark eyes, much like Syretia's grandma on her father's side.

Clara spoke about how she'd entered the essay contest at the last minute, and how the name *Curiosity* had just popped into her head. She talked about how we look up at the stars all the time, and yet we know so little about them.

"The Curiosity rover is more than just a robot," she said. "It's more than just a titanium body and aluminum wheels. Curiosity represents the hard work, passion, love, and commitment of thousands of people from all over the world who were brought together by science."

Syretia was totally mesmerized. Clara was just a little older than Syretia now, but she'd already done something that would be remembered forever.

Syretia wondered if she would ever be remembered for doing something great. Then she thought about the Geology Club she had started at her old school. Even though some kids joked that no one would join a rock collecting club, it had become really popular by the time the school year ended.

Syretia smiled at the memory, and then a pang of homesickness washed over her. Would there be kids in California who loved rocks as much as she did?

* * *

For the rest of the day, the campers gathered inside a large classroom. Counselor Tony showed a 3D model of Curiosity up on a screen.

"As many of you may know," he began, twirling a laser pointer in his hands, "this mission is called the Mars Science Laboratory, or MSL. The Curiosity rover was launched on November 26, 2011, on board an Atlas V rocket." The screen changed to show a photo of a tall, thin rocket on a launchpad.

Syretia glanced around her as Tony went on about the stages of the rocket. The other campers were glued to every word he said. She knew so little about rockets and rovers and planets. This was more Sean's subject. Syretia sighed and tried hard to pay attention.

"Curiosity is NASA's biggest rover to date," Tony went on. "It's about ten feet long and five times as heavy as the previous Mars rovers, Spirit and Opportunity." The 3D model of Curiosity appeared on the screen again. "Who can tell me about the rover's parts and why they're needed?"

Syretia could only guess that Curiosity needed six wheels to travel over the rough ground. But that was the first thing the other campers said. She hoped that Tony wouldn't call on her. Other kids said things about the

suspension system and the cameras—even one that used X-rays to examine the Martian surface.

"I read that Curiosity is different because it can collect and study rocks and minerals," Rhea said.

That made Syretia sit up straight. Rocks and minerals?

"That's exactly right," Tony said. "One of Curiosity's main goals is to study the geology of the crater it lands in." He clicked a button on his computer, and the screen lit up with words. "On the NASA website, it says: *Curiosity set out to answer the question: Did Mars ever have the right environmental conditions to support small life forms called microbes?*"

Tony paused for a moment and then said, "The answer to this question lies in the layers of rock on Mars."

Syretia was paying attention now. She knew

a lot about the types of rocks—sedimentary, igneous, and metamorphic. She knew that they told scientists a lot about the history of the planet—whether there was water, if animals had lived there, and so much more.

Syretia's thoughts buzzed with excitement. Maybe this camp would be more interesting than she'd imagined.

Chapter Three

A Lesson in Landings

Syretia was one of the first in her cabin to wake up the next morning. She realized that she was excited to see what the day would bring.

On her way to breakfast, she found her brother sitting under the big tree outside the cafeteria. His knees were pulled up to his chest, and his face was buried in his hands.

"Hey, what's up?" she asked him.

Sean rubbed his eyes with the back of his hand. "The boys in my group keep calling me 'the baby,'" he said with a hiccup. "Just because I'm still in elementary school."

"But you probably know more about space than they do," Syretia said.

"Exactly!" Sean said, brightening. "But they won't listen to any of my ideas."

Syretia huffed. Sean was a smart kid. He read tons of books about science, and especially about space. But he was small for his age, so people sometimes treated him like he was even younger.

She had an idea. "You should ask Brenda for permission to join my team." She pulled him to his feet. "We could use someone with ideas like yours."

"Really?" Sean's eyes grew wide. "You don't think I'm butting into your business?"

"Nah! Yesterday we decided to call our team the Marvelous Martians," Syretia replied. "And I think you'd fit right in."

Sean beamed as he followed his sister into the cafeteria.

* * *

It didn't take long for Sean to get a thumbs up from Brenda. By the time breakfast was over, Rhea and Cal were welcoming their new team member. And Syretia knew she'd made the right decision when they heard about their first project. It was to build a device that would protect an egg from a long drop. The team with the best-protected egg would win.

"I've done this drop contest like a million times," Rhea said as they gathered materials.

"But did you win?" Cal asked.

"No." Rhea stuck out her tongue at him. "That's why we have Syretia and Sean. They'll probably improve on my designs."

Syretia didn't know where to start. But Sean jumped right in with all kinds of ideas.

The team worked all morning, trying out everything they could think of. They finally settled on filling a toy ball with popped popcorn. Then they placed the egg in the center of the popcorn and sealed up the ball. Sean and Rhea built a parachute out of a plastic bag and strings. Cal and Syretia carefully attached the parachute to the ball.

"If this doesn't win, I don't know what will," Rhea said when they were done.

"Time's up!" Brenda called. "Let's all head to the roof."

As they gathered in the midday sun, Brenda continued. "You may be wondering why we're doing this exercise. Well, I'll let our judges explain it after they've awarded a winner." Brenda moved to the edge of the roof. The campers followed.

On the ground below, the other counselors stood around a large yellow chalk circle. Two other women, not dressed in camp T-shirts, stood with them.

"Campers, I want you to wave to our two judges," Brenda shouted so the judges would look up. "They're our special guests from JPL, here to talk to us about the Curiosity rover."

"What's JPL?" Syretia whispered to her teammates.

Sean snorted, but Rhea explained it. "JPL stands for 'Jet Propulsion Laboratory'. It's the company that builds and operates the rovers!"

Sean sighed, loudly. "JPL isn't a *company*. It's a NASA research center. It's mostly made up of researchers from the California Institute of Technology, and NASA engineers. I know this because I will be going to Caltech someday."

Syretia's eyes widened. "I had no idea you'd planned out your life that far."

"I have too!" Cal said. "Up top, little dude." He high-fived Sean, and they both laughed.

"Shh!" Rhea said. "Brenda's talking."

"Not only does your egg have to land in one piece, but it must also land within this circle," Brenda said. "The judges will choose a winner based on accuracy as well as strength of design."

Syretia's heart pounded as each team dropped its egg. Several eggs splatted as soon as they hit the concrete below. One team's parachute caught a slight breeze and landed on the grass outside the circle. Their egg survived, but it landed in the wrong place.

Now it was the Marvelous Martians' turn. Rhea had all her fingers crossed. Cal didn't have the nerve to watch. So, Sean and Syretia carried their project over to the edge and dropped their egg on the count of three.

The parachute unfolded and lifted the encased egg up slightly before floating gently downward. Syretia held her breath.

"We did it!" Sean yelled, bringing the whole team to the edge. Their device had landed just inside the edge of the yellow circle. The team watched as the judges below checked the egg. When they got a thumbs up, the team cheered. Their egg had made it!

"Did we win?" Syretia asked.

Cal shrugged. "There's only one team left to drop their egg."

"I'm keeping my fingers and arms crossed," Rhea said. Syretia joined her.

The final team—the Solar Surfers—stepped up to the edge and released their egg. With amazing accuracy, it landed unharmed, right in the middle of the circle. Syretia couldn't believe it. The perfect landing had knocked the Marvelous Martians into second place. Syretia was disappointed because they'd worked so hard. But Rhea, Cal, and even Sean still seemed happy.

"We don't want to win everything," Cal said with a shrug. "It's the Grand Project that counts the most."

"And we don't want to be the team everyone is looking to beat," Sean added.

Syretia could see their point. But this made her even more nervous about their Grand Project. What would it be? And what if they lost that too?

Chapter Four

Everyone Counts

When all the egg projects were cleaned up, the campers gathered under a large, shady tree. Brenda introduced the judges, who told everyone to call them Deb and Joss. Deb was a software engineer, and Joss was a pedologist. Syretia loved that they were both women and working on an important mission.

"What's a pedologist?" one of the campers yelled out.

"A pedologist specializes in studying soil," the woman named Joss said.

"You look at dirt all day?" Sean asked. The campers laughed.

"In a way, I do," Joss said with a smile. "Studying the soil of Mars can teach us a lot about Earth."

"That's right," Deb joined in. "Mars' surface shows us a history that has been erased on Earth by earthquakes and volcanic eruptions. These events constantly change our land and alter the record of how Earth developed."

Joss pointed to her water bottle. "And water reshapes Earth's surface even more than eruptions and quakes do."

"Through erosion!" Syretia blurted out. She slapped her hand across her mouth when she realized she'd interrupted the guests.

Joss nodded at her. "You're absolutely right. Water is a powerful force of change. But Mars has no flowing water, so its surfaces haven't been reshaped the way Earth's have. Instead, wind is the primary force of change on Mars. And without plate tectonics—to cause quakes—and no rain or flowing water, the features on Mars have not changed much over the years. In fact, some of Mars' surfaces are three or four billion years old. Studying them may help us understand how life might have started on Earth."

Syretia was so fascinated by the discussion that she quickly overcame her embarrassment at interrupting Joss. "Do you think Mars looked like Earth—with oceans and rivers and stuff—a long time ago?"

A few campers giggled, which made Syretia's embarrassment come back.

Joss shook her head. "Don't laugh. That's an excellent question." She beamed at Syretia, who turned as red as a tomato.

"We believe that Mars, billions of years ago, may have had water," Deb said. "There

are two rovers on Mars right now—Spirit and Opportunity. Their mission is to look for signs of water on Mars."

"And one of Curiosity's jobs will be to study the rocks and soil in a place that we think may have had water," Joss said. "It's called the Gale Crater. Curiosity will help us learn about whether life ever existed on Mars, and if so, how it changed the land."

Brenda appeared beside the guests. "Now that we know a little more about Curiosity's mission, maybe Deb and Joss can tell us how our egg drop challenge relates to the rover."

Deb's eyes lit up. "Each rover we send to Mars gets bigger. And that means it gets harder to land them safely. So, one challenge for the engineers at JPL was to design a better landing system for Curiosity. We can build the most advanced robot, but if it crashes on landing, all that work will have been for nothing."

The campers all nodded and murmured in agreement.

"A safe landing is not the only concern," Joss added excitedly. "Curiosity has to land inside Gale Crater, near a mountain called Mount Sharp. This area has a lot of minerals and rocks for the rover to study. But if Curiosity misses its landing spot, it might not be able to complete its mission. So, just like that circle you aimed for, Curiosity has to land in just the right spot too."

"But you have all kinds of technology you can use," Cal said, forgetting to raise his hand. "We just had straws and popcorn and stuff."

"True," Deb said. "But without creative ideas, even the best technology can't help us. We need people with imagination to be able to come up with all kinds of solutions."

"And that's why JPL is made up of so many types of scientists and engineers from all over the world," Joss said. "We need people to design, build, and even control where Curiosity will point its camera. It takes all kinds of people to operate a mission that's happening millions of miles away."

"And we also need experts to study and understand the information that Curiosity sends back to Earth." Deb patted Joss on the shoulder.

Syretia raised her hand again. "Our counselors mentioned that geologists are part of the mission too."

"That's right," Joss said. "Are you interested in rocks?"

Syretia nodded shyly.

"Did you know that there are Mars rocks on Earth?" Joss asked.

"I know that since Mars is a rocky planet like Earth, they both have igneous rocks, like basalt," Syretia replied.

"Impressive," Joss said. "But I meant actual rocks from Mars."

"I know!" Sean jumped to his feet. "Asteroids crash into Mars, breaking the planet's crust. Those broken rocks get flung into space and become meteors. When they land on Earth, they're called meteorites. And people find them all over the world."

The other campers looked at Sean in amazement. Syretia was pretty proud of her little brother.

"You're absolutely right," Joss said. "And did you know some of these meteorites were found right here in California?"

Syretia's eyes widened.

"That's right. In 1999, scientists discovered that two rocks found in the Mojave Desert were from Mars," Joss continued.

"Were they made of basalt?" Syretia couldn't help asking.

"They were," Joss said. "They are called basaltic shergottites, and they're about one hundred-eighty million years old."

"You two know a lot about rocks and meteorites," Deb said to Syretia. "Maybe someday you'll help us out in our research."

Syretia grinned. She never imagined that her love of rocks might be useful for a mission to Mars.

* * *

That night, everyone gathered in the cafeteria, and Brenda announced the details of the Grand Project.

"Okay, teams, your task is to create a dynamic presentation about Curiosity and its mission on Mars," she said. "It can be anything that shows what you've learned about the MSL. You may present it in any creative way you choose."

"Our JPL guests will return to judge your presentations," Tony added. "The winning team will get a really cool prize."

"Just think about it," Brenda said. "By the time Joss and Deb return, Curiosity will already be on Mars. The rover is scheduled to land in the next few days."

"Let's hope they're successful." Tony held up crossed fingers. All the campers did too.

Chapter Five

Seven Minutes of Suspense

The campers spent the next few days learning more about Mars and Curiosity. The teams also planned their Grand Projects.

"I think our best idea is to use the simple robotics kits they have here to build a small model of Curiosity," Rhea said.

"We could actually build it to move like a remote-control car," Cal suggested.

Sean was excited by this idea. Back in Seattle, he'd attended many robotics classes and loved building things with kits.

"I'd like to create a model of the Martian landscape and include Gale Crater using clay, paper, and paint." Syretia had done some research on the rock layers found there. "That way, we can have our Curiosity model doing its job in the precise spot it's supposed to be."

"Perfect!" Rhea said. "Let's get to work."

Syretia roped Cal into helping her while Sean and Rhea worked on the robotics. They cut open a large box to use as the base of their Martian landscape. Then they stacked thin sheets of modeling clay to make them look like the rock formations. When the clay dried, Syretia painted it to look more authentic.

"Since there might have been water on Mars at one time, I'm going to paint the deeper layers with a hint of blue," Syretia said.

"Great idea," said Cal. "And maybe we can put a small crack in the side of the crater to make it look like an old riverbed."

It was hard work that took them many hours each day. Sometimes the clay would crack or crumble and they'd have to start again. But they didn't give up.

While Cal finished off the outer layers, Syretia created a round basin to represent Gale Crater, where Curiosity was to explore.

"It won't quite be to scale," Syretia said when Rhea and Sean brought their partially built rover model over to compare it to the crater. "Obviously, the real crater would be much larger than the rover, but we don't have a box big enough."

Sean patted her on the back. "It's absolutely splendid!" He spoke like an old professor, and everyone laughed.

As the campers became more involved with their projects, the counselors found it harder and harder to pull them away for other activities. Nobody wanted to leave their projects, and everyone kept theirs a secret from the rest of the campers.

With time running out, the Marvelous Martians really pulled together. Syretia helped Rhea paint the details on the Curiosity model. Meanwhile, Sean and Cal collected pebbles around camp. Then they placed them in their crater for the robot to lift.

Finally—on the night before their presentations—they decided they were finished. Standing back to look at their work, the team grinned at their model robot rover sitting in its Martian landscape.

"We're sure to win the competition this year," Rhea proclaimed.

That night, Syretia returned to her cabin exhausted but happy. As Brenda turned out the lights, there was excited chatter about Curiosity's landing. Word had gotten around that it was happening sometime that night.

"No more talking," Brenda said with a wink. "We'll hear all about it in the morning."

Syretia felt as if her head had just touched the pillow when the pod lights suddenly came on again.

"Get up quickly, girls. We have a surprise," Brenda said. "We're going to listen in as Curiosity lands."

That announcement got the campers up fast. They hurried through the dark to the cafeteria. The screen was being prepared as Syretia joined her team.

"Listen carefully, everyone," Brenda said. "We'll be watching the JPL control room on YouTube as their engineers monitor Curiosity's landing in real time."

The screen lit up, showing people sitting in rows in front of computer screens. They were all dressed in blue shirts, and most wore headphones. Occasionally, a lady asked questions and a man with a headset explained what was happening.

As the campers watched, Tony put up another screen. It showed an animation to help them understand the landing.

"Of course, we can't watch the landing in real life, since no one is out there to film it," Brenda said, chewing on her thumbnail.

Syretia sensed that *everyone* was nervous. They all wanted this landing to be a success.

"They're now starting the EDL—entry, descent, and landing stages," Brenda explained. "From the time Curiosity enters the atmosphere to the moment it lands takes about seven minutes. In that time, it must slow from thirteen thousand miles an hour to zero."

"It's called the seven minutes of terror," Tony said. "Because so much could go wrong."

Syretia gasped. This mission sounded almost impossible.

"But they'll have a parachute to slow it down," Cal said as he watched the animation.

"Yes, and it's the largest parachute ever built," Tony said. "Yet it will only slow Curiosity down to two hundred miles an hour. It needs to be slower than that to land safely."

"That's where the Sky Crane comes in," Brenda went on. "It's a device that holds on to Curiosity until it's close to the planet's surface. Then it fires small rockets to slow itself down."

On the video animation, the Sky Crane fired its rockets as it got closer to the ground. Then the rover was lowered using a bunch of wires. When Curiosity touched down, the wires cut off and the crane swooshed away.

"Now that you've watched the animation," Brenda said, "you'll be able to understand what's going on in the JPL video."

The campers sat on the edge of their seats as they listened to the last few minutes of

the broadcast. It felt as if everything was happening in slow motion.

"Sky Crane has started," someone at JPL said. Another man paced back and forth across the screen, making Syretia feel even more nervous.

Minutes went by, and no announcements were made. The people at JPL stared at their screens. Syretia could practically feel the tension—both in the cafeteria and at JPL. If Curiosity crashed, everything that had gone into the mission would be lost.

Rhea drummed her fingers on the table.

"Why isn't anyone saying anything?" Syretia whispered.

"Curiosity should have landed by now," Sean said, checking his watch.

The people on the video grew very quiet. So did the campers. Syretia could hear her own heartbeat.

Suddenly, a huge cheer erupted from the people at JPL. They jumped out of their seats and hugged each other. All over the cafeteria, campers clapped and whooped too. Curiosity had landed safely!

It was the most exciting night Syretia had ever experienced. As she and her teammates walked back to their pods, they looked up at the stars.

Sean pointed. "Isn't it beautiful?" he said. "On a clear night like tonight, I feel like I could reach out and touch the stars!"

"Think about it. Out there, Curiosity is just beginning its historic journey," Rhea whispered as she linked her arm with Syretia's. "And we got to be a part of it."

"Good night, little rover," Syretia whispered as she headed back into her pod. "Stay safe."

* * *

The next morning, Deb and Joss arrived to cheers from the campers. No one was nervous about their presentations because they were all so excited about Curiosity's success.

The cafeteria space was cleared so that teams could set up their projects around the room. Team members waited for the judges to come by and listen to their presentations.

Deb and Joss walked over to the Marvelous Martians' table. They studied the display of the Martian landscape.

"Our model represents a small section of the Gale Crater," Syretia explained as Rhea switched on their rover. The model crept like a slow ant across the landscape. "It shows the type of terrain Curiosity is exploring."

"Excellent work," Joss said.

"Well done!" Deb said as she jotted notes. "I love all the small details—from the rock layers to the movable limbs on the rover."

As they waited for the judges' decisions, Syretia turned to Rhea. "I don't even mind if we lose this contest. Watching Curiosity land safely was enough for me."

"Not for me," Rhea said. "I want to win!"

An hour later, Brenda's microphone squealed, and everyone went silent.

"The judges have made their decision," Brenda began. "You should all be proud of the amazing work you've done."

"Okay, but who won?" Cal shouted. The whole room burst into laughter.

Brenda handed her microphone to Deb. "It was a tough decision," she said. "I believe you've all learned that it takes many people with all kinds of talents to make a project like MSL work. You all impressed us a lot, but one team stood out."

"That's right," Joss leaned in and spoke into the microphone too. "Drum roll please . . ."

Campers drummed their hands on any surface they could find.

"The winners are the Marvelous Martians!"

Syretia could hardly believe it. She'd never won anything before. Their prize was a special T-shirt designed by Brenda and autographed by Deb and Joss.

"When you come back next year, you can wear this as a reminder of your win," Brenda said as she presented Syretia with her T-shirt.

"Are we coming back next year?" Sean asked, turning to his sister.

"You have to come back!" Rhea shrieked. "We'll share a bunk and be best friends."

Syretia gave her new friend a hug. She was so glad that she'd come to this camp. California was starting to feel a little more like home.

THE HISTORY BEHIND THE MARS ROVERS

NASA and the Jet Propulsion Laboratory (JPL) have sent several rovers to Mars. The first one was named Sojourner. It launched on December 4, 1996, and was part of the Mars Pathfinder mission. Its job was to send close-up images and data from rocks near the landing site back to Earth. Sojourner spent 83 days on Mars before it stopped working.

Spirit and Opportunity were the next rovers sent to Mars. Spirit launched on June 10, 2003, and Opportunity launched on July 7, 2003. They landed in places where scientists suspected water had existed on Mars in the past. Their mission was to learn more about the history of water on the planet and find out how long ago it had flowed on Mars' surface.

Curiosity was launched on November 26, 2011, as part of the Mars Science Laboratory (MLS) mission. The rover landed inside Gale Crater on August 5, 2012. Its goals were to investigate Martian climate and geology.

Curiosity was the largest rover sent to Mars at the time. It was about the size of a small car, and as tall as a basketball player. It carried many science instruments, including 17 cameras, a laser to vaporize rocks, and a drill to collect powdered rock samples. It looked for rocks that contained signs that water or microbial life had existed on the planet millions of years ago.

In September 2014, Curiosity began its journey to climb Mount Sharp, a 3-mile- (4.8-km-) high mountain. As it climbed, it studied the mountain's layers of sedimentary rock. According to the NASA website, *"[e]ach layer helps tell the story about how Mars changed from being more Earth-like—with lakes, streams and a thicker atmosphere—to the nearly-airless, freezing desert it is today."*

The MSL mission has been a huge success for NASA. It has proven that it is possible to land a large, heavy rover safely and accurately in a specific area on another planet. It has also given scientists and engineers on Earth the ability to study another planet from afar because the rover could study samples and then send the data to computers on Earth.

NASA's latest rover is named Perseverance. It launched on July 30, 2020, and landed on Mars on February 18, 2021. Perseverance is looking for signs of life by studying parts of Mars that might have had lakes or rivers. It carries with it many advanced instruments that can take rock samples and look for tiny fossils or signs of ancient life on Mars. It also carries the first Mars Helicopter with it. This helicopter is called Ingenuity, and it is powered by its own solar panels. Ingenuity allows scientists to remotely fly short distances over Mars to give them even more information about the Red Planet.

GLOSSARY

atmosphere (AT-muh-sfeer)—the layer of gases that surrounds some planets, dwarf planets, and moons

erosion (ih-ROH-zhuhn)—the wearing away of land by water or wind

geology (jee-AHL-uh-jee)—the study of minerals, rocks, and soil

igneous (IG-nee-uhss)—relating to rock that was once melted, but then cooled and hardened

metamorphic (met-uh-MOR-fik)—relating to rock that is changed by heat and pressure

meteor (MEE-tee-ur)—a rock or dust that enters Earth's atmosphere, causing a streak of light

meteorite (MEE-tee-ur-rite)—a piece of meteor that falls all the way to the ground

microbe (MYE-krobe)—a living thing that is too small to see without a microscope

mineral (MIN-ur-uhl)—a substance found in nature that is not made by a plant or animal

pedologist (ped-AHL-uh-jist)—a scientist who studies soil and the materials it contains

sedimentary (sed-uh-MEN-tuh-ree)—relating to rock formed by layers of rocks, sand, or clay that have been pressed together

ACTIVITY

Have an Egg Drop Challenge!

Challenge your friends to build a device that protects an egg from splatting when it falls from a great height.

What You Need:

- raw eggs

- tape, glue, or other sticky things

- scissors

- recycled or reusable materials such as cardboard, craft foam, balloons, popcorn, packing peanuts, craft sticks, string, cotton, wool, straws, tissue paper, sponges, and plastic bags

- pencil and paper